GRUFF GARRETT LAWDOG

THE OLD NEMESIS

JOHN J. LAW

Chapter One: Ending on A High Note

Gruff Garrett, the old lawdog sat in the train car and took a look through the window. The scenery passed by in front of him, as the train roared over the tracks. Inside the train car, Gruff noticed how fast everything seemed to be passing him by. The trees, the animals grazing or running by, and the houses that dotted the landscape all seemed to move like a blur through the window. Gruff had traveled around with his old roan Dynamite before, but this was only his third time on a train. He had never really considered just how fast and efficient these large, metal boxes were. It was a profound moment for an old lawdog like himself to consider.

"Everything's passin' by, just like a dream." he muttered to himself.

Gruff had to consider the moment, and savor it. He wanted to hold the moment in both hands and stop time somehow. An old man himself would surely want time to stand still even for... a moment. Everything just seemed to be moving so fast for Gruff these days, and he would do anything to just slow things down. Perhaps smoking some tobacco would help.

Gruff took out a cheap cigar from his shirt pocket. It was the same pocket he kept his heart starting medicine in. Gruff ignored the blatantly ironic fact that he kept his medicine and his cigar in the same pocket. One was there to keep him alive in case of an emergency, and the other was there to give him pleasure, but could also endanger him. He vaguely remembered his doctor warning him about smoking too much and how such a habit could only make his already weak ticker worse.

Gruff could still hear Doc Wingham at the back of his head.

"You've got a weak ticker, Gruff. You should really stop smoking them tobacco sticks of yers. Maybe even stop drinking too, if you can. All that stuff's bad for the heart."

"Doc, if yer askin' me to stop smokin' and drinkin' yer pretty much askin' me to stop livin'."

Doc Wingham chuckled when he heard Gruff's stubborn, but not unexpected answer. Gruff was an old patient of his, and he pretty much knew what to expect from the old lawdog by now. That included a general mistrust of doctors like himself.

"Heh. I ain't askin' ya to stop yer habits, Gruff. No one can order a man to do something he don't wanna do. It's still your life. But don't say I didn't warn ya."

Gruff didn't argue with Doc Wingham. He appreciated that the doc wasn't the nagging type. Gruff was still concerned with the Doc's ominous warning. He just tried to hide his concern from everyone else, including himself.

"Doc askin' me to stop smokin' an' drinkin'? What's an old geezer like myself supposed to do? Old habits die hard, I say!"

Gruff took a moment to pause and look at the shapes that the smoke from his cigar produced. He allowed his mind to wander and interpret the shapes as whatever he thought they represented. He saw a horse, a gun, and even the outlines of a face. He couldn't be sure what the features looked like though. The smoke was just too hazy to make out a clear and recognizable face. He wasn't sure why, but he suddenly remembered Katie Kemp. Perhaps it was because the smoke was too hazy and obscure, so his mind simply focused on Katie's face, as it was the most recognizable right now. It was the most recognizable not for any fond memory, but for the trauma and shock it caused Gruff.

Gruff tried to push her image out of his mind but he couldn't. It was too late. He remembered how he had just been holding her hand, and the two of them had been walking down the main road on the small town of Cascade. They were enjoying the early morning of a new day, and were about to try some Chinese food. The day had seemed so promising. Neither of them expected what happened next.

It was Gruff who spotted something wrong while they were walking past the small town's bank. Gruff noticed the unhitched horses in front of the bank. Seconds later, the gunmen came running out of the bank's front door. Gruff told Katie to run towards a nearby water barrel, he noticed earlier. It was while Katie was running towards the water barrel that disaster struck.

One of the bank robbers fired at Gruff. He later realized that he probably fired at him because of the badge he was still sporting. The shot missed him but struck Katie who was still running for the barrel.

Gruff tried to return fire and actually managed to shoot one of the bank robbers. However, his retaliation was stopped abruptly when he felt something tighten around his chest. He would later recall that it felt like a small fist constricting and squeezing his heart. It was a very untimely heart attack.

Gruff tried to fire his gun, but the pain was too great. He couldn't even stand, and he collapsed as the bank robbers rode away with their loot. He survived when one of the responding cops of the small town managed to give him his heart medicine, but he would never forget Katie's tragic and senseless death. Katie had been killed by a bullet meant for him, and it cut Gruff deep in his heart.

After the terrible incident, Gruff's Chief Marshal Howard Longsdale visited him at his home, but it wasn't a social call. Howard came to his house to personally enforce his own retirement upon Gruff. Howard had always been a lenient boss, and a longtime friend, and he had always put off this forced retirement on Gruff. After all, Gruff was a friend and a peer. They were of the same age range, and Gruff had always proven himself in his work to be just as, or even more capable than most young men. How could he enforce it upon Gruff? The man had proven his worth so far.

Howard wanted to enforce it, this time. After all, it was clear that the death of Katie Kemp deeply affected Gruff. This was quite unusual, but Howard didn't judge Gruff. Katie was only a lady in waiting that Gruff had met in the small town of Cascade. They were not in any kind of deep relationship. For all intents and purposes, she was only a girl that Gruff had briefly met and enjoyed a casual encounter with. Despite this, her death had affected the old marshal a lot more than what was expected.

It was for this reason that Howard thought it would have been best to retire Gruff, but it wasn't going to happen. Gruff pleaded Howard to keep him as a marshal for one last job. Gruff begged Howard not to let him go, saying his last memory couldn't be one where he saw Katie die like that. Like most old veterans, Gruff wanted to go on a high note.

It was an understandable sentiment, and Howard wasn't surprised. Gruff realized only now that Howard must have expected him to plead for one last job.

"Howard must have expected that I wouldn't just want to retire so easily. I could never get one over that wily old coot. Kind of reminds of myself actually. Howard was expecting it, so he gave me this assignment so easily."

Gruff was back in the present now. His mind tossed the memories aside and his eyes wandered down on the folder and the files that were on his lap. They were files of his most recent assignment, the assignment he was on right now.

It was a routine enough assignment, something Gruff could do with his eyes closed. He could see why Howard would toss this assignment on his lap. It was so simple that even an old marshal like himself could do it so easily. Not that Gruff had a bad record or anything. He had a sterling record he could be proud of. No, it wasn't that Howard was afraid he would mess this assignment up. It was more of something so routine and mandatory that Gruff would easily be able to end his long and illustrious career in law enforcement on that high note he wanted so badly. That was probably what Howard was thinking when he gave Gruff the assignment. Gruff wasn't sure if he found this comforting or insulting. Either way, it didn't matter. He had his final assignment now, and he would finish it.

The assignment was simple enough. An old outlaw by the name of John B. Bryan had been apprehended by an old bounty hunter Monty Mathers down in Blue Rock. It was a considerable distance to Blue Rock so Gruff had to take a train to get to the destination. Mathers was holding Bryan in a cell there, waiting for Gruff to pick him up, and send him to a proper holding area. A simple pick up of an apprehended felon. It was a simple enough job for an old timer like Gruff Garrett.

Gruff continued to smoke on his cheap cigar, enjoying each whiff and puff. The old lawdog found it quite satisfying to smoke while contemplating past events like this. He did not even consider the fact that there were other passengers seated in front of him, two women. It was clear that both of them did not approve of Gruff's smoking, but he didn't seem to care much about the inconvenience he was causing.

"Of all the most rotten and insensitive things! Puff your smoke elsewhere!"

"Aunt Betsy's right, old man! Didn't you notice that it ain't polite to smoke in an enclosed space like this? Then again, I didn't figure an old geezer like yourself knew anything about manners!"

The younger lady was clearly a lot more hostile towards Gruff. Perhaps it was her youth, or perhaps she was simply annoyed at the old lawdog's own blatant insensitivity.

"Oh, I'm sorry. I didn't know I was offending you ladies' delicate sensibilities an' all."

Gruff sounded more than a little sarcastic, and the two ladies did not appreciate this. Despite the sarcasm, Gruff made an effort to puff the smoke out through the train's open window. It was a lot of effort for a crass old man like himself. Aunt Betsy and her niece however, did not seem to appreciate it.

"Aunt Betsy, have you heard of the sasquatch?" the young lady said.

"No, Anna. I can't say that I have. You must have read about this how do you say it? This 'sasquatch' from all the books you read."

Anna smiled and smirked. She took pride in the fact that she read a lot and knew many little details most people did not.

"It's a mythical creature from many of the savage cultures. A lot of the savages say that it's a man who practiced cannibalism and as a result was punished by the spirits for his transgression."

Aunt Betsy looked very appalled at the very mention of cannibalism.

"They don't approve of cannibalism? I verily thought that they all practiced as such! They are all truly savages, after all!"

Gruff heard the two women speaking and was not

pleased. An old lawdog like himself had more than his fair share of encounters with various Indians. He knew from experience that these people were not the "savages" that most of the white folk like himself viewed them as. Gruff was one of many others who viewed them in a different way. Experience had taught him that they were also very intelligent, had their own culture, and basically had just as much foibles as the next person. They were just unfortunately in the way of good old Manifest Destiny and American expansion. Such talk as Aunt Betsy and Anna were having only showed how much discrimination and disrespect were very rampant.

"I'll let you know that them Indians ain't 'savages' as you ladies put it!" Gruff said.

He couldn't help but interrupt them now, but the two ladies ignored his response. They carried on with their discussion as if Gruff had not said anything.

"Like I said, the sasquatch is said to be one of their own who strayed and practiced cannibalism. He is usually identified by his large size and shaggy appearance, usually akin to that of an unshaven and hairy gorilla."

Anna glared at Gruff. "Apparently a sasquatch seems to be sitting right in front of us. Or at least someone who looks quite similar to one. We should be wary of this one." Anna said.

Aunt Betsy couldn't help herself now. She tried to keep from laughing, but she could not. Her face displayed a long and wide grin that eventually became a soft chuckle that grew to a modest laugh. Anna looked at Gruff again with a look that was not dripping with contempt now, but seemed actually mildly amused.

"Ah, Anna! You do have a great sense of wit about you. Truly you can make the most unbearable experiences bearable and even a trifle amusing." Aunt Betsie said.

Gruff nodded and smiled at the two women. The joke was at his expense, but he would not allow himself to be affected. The old lawdog simply tossed aside his now spent cigar out the window. Once that was done, he promptly got up from his seat and grabbed his saddlebags, tossing them on his shoulder as he did so.

Gruff displayed unusual strength for his age, and looked over the two women, as he got up. Anna, the well-read one, could have passed as his granddaughter. Aunt Betsie seemed to be at least as old and worn as he was. If they hadn't been so rude, Gruff might have enjoyed some conversation with them, but that was not to be.

"I can see that I'm not wanted and neither of you fine ladies cannot appreciate the perspective of an old lawdog like myself. That being said, I shall enjoy another cigar elsewhere on this train in private. And one more thing, neither of you are ladies, and neither of you are definitely fine."

Gruff turned his back on Aunt Betsie and Anna. He did not notice both women glaring at him, giving him the dirtiest look they could. One of them seemed to have thrown some kind of obscenity that was directed at Gruff, but he could not be sure. Either way, Gruff didn't care. He just wanted to be as far away from the two "ladies" as he could be.

Gruff made his way to the vestibule in between cars. Gruff was outside now, and the wind blew past him, even as he heard the roar of the train's metal wheels rolling on the metal tracks. The scenery outside seemed to fly past Gruff even faster, now that he was outside.

He held on to the vestibule's railing with one hand, while taking out another cigar. Despite his advanced age, Gruff did not struggle to keep his balance as he stood on the vestibule. He easily lit the cigar and enjoyed the smoke, undisturbed for the rest of the journey.

Gruff didn't notice the time pass, and soon train screeched to a halt. All the cars stopped as the locomotive took water in a small depot. The conductor and the brakemen took the time to smoke themselves. Gruff was familiar with the small depot, and he knew this was stop. Gruff got off the car, and made his way to the stable car where the horses were. He led his old roan Dynamite down the loading ramp from the stable car. Gruff held old Dynamite's reins gently and the old roan trotted with its master. Dynamite had seen a lot of action with Gruff and a bond between man and beast had long been formed. Both Gruff and his roan were old but still very capable. It was almost as if the horse and the man were extensions of each other.

Gruff had led his horse a short distance when he saw the short, and pudgy black man in front of him. The man was in charge of the depot where the train had stopped.

Gruff saw him and both men recognized each other instantly.

"Been a while eh, Quincy?" Gruff said.

Quincy Pearson smiled at Gruff. The two men had known each other from way back. Quincy had always lived out here in the middle of nowhere and worked for the railroad company managing the small depot for as long as Gruff could remember. The depot was Quincy's home, and he was a familiar face that Gruff saw every time he passed by, which hadn't been in a while.

Gruff could still remember a time when Quincy wasn't as old and ancient as he was now. The same could be said about Quincy remembering Gruff in much younger days, as well. Both men could still remember when there were much less gray hairs on their heads. Both of them could still remember a time when they were much stronger and when life seemed just a little bit more hopeful than it was now.

"Been too long since you passed by this way, old man!" Quincy said, laughing with good nature.

"Speak for yourself old timer, heh! I'm glad to see you're still down here by the depot even after all these years."

Quincy shrugged his shoulders.

"Heheh. Where else am I supposed to go? You know how it is, Gruff. Us old timers we're like crab grass. Once we've set our roots in, it's hard to pull us outta the ground."

Gruff nodded. He could understand what Quincy meant perfectly.

"I can definitely agree with that, Quincy. They sure want to pull me outta the service, but I'm hangin' on."

"Henry still the Chief Marshal?"

"It's Howard, Quincy. And yes, he's still the chief marshal."

Quincy scratched the back of his head with more than a little embarrassment.

"Dang! It's Howard, yeah. Howard Longsdale. That's

another old weed like us. When you reach this age, it gets kinda harder to remember little details like first names an' such."

"Tell me all about it. Well, Howard sent me down to Blue Rock to pick up an outlaw by the name of John B. Bryan. It's a simple pick up."

"Blue Rock? That's a short ride from here. You're picking up and escorting a prisoner back to the other marshals? Man, time must definitely be catching up to you, Gruff. Time was once that you could handle much tougher assignments than a simple pick up."

Gruff shrugged his shoulders.

"It's called growing old, Quincy. Father time catches up with all of us. Present company included."

"Heh. Guess you're right there, Gruff. You don't look so thrilled to be doing this job. Considering your age an' how simple it is, I'm guessing, this could be your last job?"

"It is my last job, Quincy. Howard and I agreed to as much. If it were up to me, I sure would have wanted to keep on workin' but it's not. I guess I should be happy. It's been a long run for me, a lot longer than most marshals."

"You bet you should be happy, Gruff! Bein' a lawman ain't an easy job. A lotta lawmen don't reach your age. A lotta 'em well, they die young. Hazards of the job an' all."

"I'm well aware of the fact that I'm probably livin' a lot longer than I deserve, Quincy. It's been a long and rewarding career for me, but I still wish I could go a little longer."

Quincy waved a hand at Gruff.

"Ah, I guess it's just human nature. Most men just don't know when to call it quits. Me? I'm lookin' forward to retiring and staying somewhere else besides this small depot."

"Good for you, Quincy. I reckon you were able to save up a little of your salary for retirement?"

"You could say that, yeah. If I were to retire now, I could probably spend the last of days starin' at pretty girls pass me by. And that day's probably comin' a lot sooner than I think too."

Quincy smiled, revealing several rows of yellowed

teeth. His teeth were colored pale yellow from so much misuse and tobacco chewing and smoking, but he still had a full set of them. This was still quite the achievement in the current times.

"Just watchin' pretty girls pass you by? I sure couldn't take that. If a pretty girl passed me by, I sure would want to do something more than just stare at her."

"Heh. I never did have a knack for women like you do, Gruff. Me? I've always just been a simple sort, just happy to get by day to day an' all."

"Believe me Quincy. Sometimes bein' alone is a lot better n' bein' with a pretty lady."

It was a surprisingly pensive answer to Quincy's light-hearted observation. Gruff couldn't help but feel this way. The mention of women drew Gruff's mind back to the memory of Katie Kemp and her terrible death, just over a week ago. Her death was still fresh in the old lawdog's mind and still affected him greatly.

"Sound like you got somethin' on yer mind? Or someone?"

"You could say that. But I'm getting too old to

ruminate about the past. But then again, maybe ruminating and looking back are the only things old men like us can do. I got a prisoner to pick up, Quincy. I do hope you enjoy your coming retirement a lot more than I'm enjoying mine."

With that, Gruff turned around with his roan, and started to walk away. Quincy stood where he was and watched as the old marshal slowly began to walk towards the horizon, to the path that led to Blue Rock. Quincy felt bad for his old friend. The old marshal sounded quite tired and weary and it was clear that the years had taken their toll on him. Quincy couldn't help but wonder if as he stared at Gruff walking away, that perhaps he was not just staring at Gruff. Perhaps he was also staring at a cracked reflection of himself as well.

It was a sobering thought, and Quincy was lost to it, in the moment. Perhaps he would not be so pensive if he knew that other, unwelcome eyes were watching him just as he was watching Gruff.

"Is that who I think it was?" one of the men asked.

One of the other men nodded. "That's him all right.

That's Gruff Garrett. A little more weathered and beaten than I last remembered him. But that's the man. I can't forget a face as ugly as Garrett's. Especially after what he did to us. That old man owes us a whole lot."

The men came from the loading car and rode the train, just like Gruff. They had also gotten down at the depot, unloading their own mares from the stable car, as well. These men were following Gruff.

"Tell me about it, Spike. He landed us all in the slammer for that old job back in Hucksville. Seems like ages ago now, and we lost six months of our lives rotting in that prison before we managed to break out."

The anger and resentment from the men's voices were palpable. These were the Dunlevy boys. Spike, Bubba, and Devin were three outlaw brothers who had gained an infamous reputation as merciless robbers and murderers. They had committed a series of bank robberies in the neighboring territories for some time before Garrett had caught them and sent them to jail. Their sentences were much longer, but they managed to break out of prison in a general prison riot. All this happened many years ago, and the Dunlevy brothers never expected to bump into Gruff Garrett like this. Unfortunately for Gruff, their paths met now. He just didn't know it. Now, the three men had an axe to grind with the old marshal, and they were determined to make him pay.

"I honestly thought we would never bump into Garrett again after all these years. When I spotted him at the train station, I didn't even recognize him at first." Spike said.

"The years made him look even uglier than he already was." Bubba said.

"Indeed. Well, looks ain't going to be an issue when he's six feet under! But who knows? Maybe he'll carry those ugly looks of his into the afterlife." Devin said.

"He probably will. Anyways, an old coot like that's lived long enough. It's time we put down that ugly dog once and for all. We better keep at him."

"You boys talkin' about Gruff Garrett?"

The Dunlevy boys turned and saw the old and pudgy Quincy Pearson standing in front of them. The old, black man asked them straight up and didn't seem intimidated in the least bit by the three men.

"Yeah, so we are. What's it to you, mister?" Spike said.

He stared straight at Quincy with much contempt. Quincy stared right back at the Dunlevy boys' leader and did not flinch.

"Nothing much, really. Gruff's just as old and ancient as I am. Used to see him a lot come down here at the depot

when we were a lot younger. Now, he's just old an' fulla warts and wrinkles."

"Exactly. You got a lot a stones approaching us like you did, old timer. Don't you know who we are?" Spike said.

Quincy shrugged his shoulders. "No, should I? I'm just here managing the depot an' all. Far as I can tell you boys have some kinda' beef with Gruff, am I right?"

It was Bubba who answered Quincy. "You bet we got a beef with the old lawdog, mister. He owes us, big time, an' me an' my brothers intend for him to pay all of it to us. In full."

"Heh. With interest too, actually." Devin added.

With the tone of their voices, Quincy could tell that these boys were planning nothing good for Gruff. Despite this, he didn't seem too concerned.

"Maybe you boys oughtta take it easy with Gruff. He's as old as I am. The old timer can't hurt you boys more'n you can hurt him. Can't see how an' old geezer like him could be a threat to you boys."

"Oh you would be surprised at how crazy that old fart could be, mister. You would be very surprised."

Quincy nodded. "I guess you're right about that. It's kind of amazing that he's even lived this long."

Spike smirked as he clenched a fist. "Well, me and my brothers gonna make sure to give him a good sendoff to the next life."

"I'm beggin' y'all boys. Gruff's an old timer. He can barely tell right from left or even his own name sometimes. He's just out there, already. He can't do nuthin' to you no more. Please just let him go." Quincy said.

Spike shook his head. "Can't do that, old timer. Garrett's done too much to answer for. Come on boys. We've wasted enough time

chatting here. Best we catch up to that old geezer and finish him off."

With that the Dunlevy brothers saddled up on their horses and rode away. They left to follow Gruff and to ambush him. Quincy was left standing by the depot alone. He watched as the three young outlaws rode off and disappeared into the horizon. A smile broke out of his face, revealing his yellow teeth again.

"Heh. You boys can try to take down Gruff all right. But don't say I didn't warn you. For an old dog, Gruff still got a really bad bite." he said.

Chapter Two: A Change of Heart

The three men followed Gruff's racks down through Stone Cold canyon, a wide gap of nothing but rocks and dirt between limestone and sandstone peaks. The gap was cut by a deep river that rushed down the area eons ago, when Gruff and the Dunlevy's and everyone else were not even concepts. The land was much different then, and no men lived through those times to tell the tale. It was a rough and rocky path, but the three brothers stuck with it, determined to catch up to, and ambush Gruff Garrett.

It was Devin who voiced some apprehension about their plan.

"Is this all worth it, Spike? I mean, following Garrett through these rough trails is tough, but what if that Blackie by the depot was right? What if Garrett's senile and not himself no more? Where would the satisfaction be in killing an old man like that?" he asked.

"Are you forgettin' that this senile old man was the reason we languished in the clink for six months? An' we could have stayed there longer, if that massive jail breakout didn't happen." Spike said.

There was more than a hint of annoyance in Spike Dunlevy's voice. Being the eldest, he was the leader of his siblings, and he didn't like being questioned like that.

"I ain't sayin' I forgot our hard time in the slammer, Spike. I just meant..."

"If you really hadn't forgotten those six months, you wouldn't be questioning why we have to kill him." Spike said.

"Spike's right, Devin. I sure didn't appreciate that dumb marshal stopping us from robbing that bank in West Bakerton."

"You're both right, an' like our time at the slammer, I still remember Garrett foiling that West Bakerton job. We rode with some other boys back then, but he managed to take them all out and haul us back to a judge. I can't forget any of that, and he's gonna pay for all that time we spent in the slammer!"

Bubba and Spike Dunlevy were committed to taking out the old marshal, but it was Devin who had his doubts about all this.

"I don't have any love lost for that old geezer too. I

just can't shake the feeling that something ain't right. I get the feeling that we're all in a lot of danger here." Devin said.

Spike and Bubba laughed hard at their sibling's fears. Their laughter echoed through the canyon.

"You heard that Spike? Little brother Devin's really got a bad case of a yellow belly this time!" Bubba said.

"Yeah, Devin. Come on and grow a pair, will you? You saw how old Garrett is. At his age, it's a crime that he's even still in the force. He probably begged for his job. Ain't no way an old fossil like that can stand up to the three of us!"

Spike spoke with total confidence, but Devin was still not inspired. The tension was clearly written all over his face.

"I don't know. This is the man that put us away in the slammer in the first place here. And what if he's been a marshal for so long, not because he begged for some favors but because he is genuinely competent? What if that's just how efficient he is, and that's why they can't just boot him off the force? If that's the case we should be extra careful and...”

“We already are extra careful! It's not like we're announcing our presence to him, are we?”

Spike spoke with clear annoyance in his voice now. It was clear that he didn't fancy his younger brother doubting their own competence.

“You ask me Devin; you're giving this old fossil too much credit! He's old and way past his prime! This isn't the same man that put us away years ago! Honestly, I never thought I would ever bump into his old sorry ass again. When the years passed by like that, I thought we had all passed up our chance at retribution a long time ago. But when I saw the old geezer board that train, I knew we had to tag along and follow him. I didn't even recognize him at first because he was so old. He looked like an old raisin; I could barely tell it was the same marshal that took us in. But it was him all right. It was Gruff Garrett. I could tell by them eyes of his. Those eyes still had that look of self-righteousness they did all those years ago. When I realized it was Garrett, I just had to drag all of us into that train to follow him to God knows where! This was a one in a million chance that I wasn't gonna pass up!"

It was clear that Spike was not going to let the chance to take down Gruff pass them by. He was not going to be dissuaded from what they had to do, just because Devin was getting anxious. Devin simply did not say anything anymore after Spike's rant. He knew by now that there was no point in arguing with him now.

"Why the marshals would even allow that old coot to go down such rough terrain like this is beyond me. Someone that old ought shouldn't even be fit to ride around in rough country like this. That old goat really must have friends in high places to still even be working up to now!"

Devin thought that perhaps the fact that Gruff was still going down such a rough terrain and handling this kind of work only showed how much faith the marshals still had in him. This, despite his advanced age, could only mean that perhaps the old marshal was a lot more dangerous than Spike and Bubba were giving him credit for. Devin didn't say as much, but he was still very worried about all of this. Perhaps they were underestimating the old lawdog a little too much. Devin was very concerned, but he didn't dare say it out loud. Spike was already getting annoyed with him, and he didn't want to get under his older brother's skin. Devin didn't like Spike when he was angry.

The three men rode a little more down the gap in the canyon, a little past sunset. Darkness was slowly covering the land when they caught sight and scent of something.

"Do you smell that boys?" Spike said.

"I think I do, big brother." Bubba said.

"What do you smell?" Devin asked.

"As always, you're so slow, little brother. Didn't ya pick up the scent?"

Skip and Bubba both caught whiff of it. Their sense of smell, like their other senses were heightened to an unusual degree. This was because of all the time they had spent in the outdoors, evading the law, or engaging in life and death gunfights. With a lifestyle like that, they always had to be ready for anything, and their senses were always on alert, for even the slightest hints of interest or danger.

"It's the whiff of coffee in the air. Freshly brewed too." Spike said.

"I smell it too, Spike! Someone's brewing coffee, or has brewed it close by."

"Do you see it there in the distance? That faint light?"

It was Devin who spotted it now. The faintest hint of a lit fire in the distance. Perhaps Gruff Garrett was close by now.

"I see the light! That old lawdog must be camped over there! Everybody get off yer horses and let's move forward real slow! We should also try to move as quietly as possible and whisper." Spike said.

Spike's two brothers were quick to comply with his orders. They all alighted from their horses with surprising ease and with minimal noise. They hitched the horses by some trees and when they were sure the horses were secure, they began to slowly and quietly creep towards the light in the distance.

The three men approached the light in the distance, as quietly as they could. They crouched on the ground to stay low, and moved slowly and cautiously. They made sure their boots made as little noise as possible. The men gripped their drawn revolvers tightly, each of them ready to fire at a moment's notice.

Eventually, they got close enough to confirm that the light was indeed coming from a campfire. The flames danced around the firewood, crackling and silently illuminating the Dunlevy brothers' approach. That was not the only thing it illuminated. Right in front of the campfire was a prone figure. The figure was wrapped in a blanket with a tipped hat over his head. The head was resting on a large saddlebag for a pillow.

The three men immediately recognized this as Gruff Garrett. The three men silently nodded at each other, knowing that Garrett was lying in front of them peacefully in slumber. The also knew that the slightest noise might alert the old lawdog right now, and it was best to stay quiet for just a little longer.

Spike Dunlevy silently met the gaze of Bubba and

Devin. There was a look of excitement and anticipation in his eyes. The anticipation was mixed with grit and focus. Spike didn't need to say a word. His brothers understood immediately that he was determined to extend Garrett's slumber to eternity.

Spike carefully aimed his gun and pulled the chamber back. The revolver was well-oiled and pulling back the chamber made the slightest click, but someone would have to be wide awake and with exceptional senses to hear it. Garrett had the latter, but he was too deep in slumber to hear it. Spike looked at his brothers one last time. Devin and Bubba nodded silently and acknowledged Spike, as they also pulled out their weapons and readied them to fire. Their guns were all pointed squarely at the slumbering marshal.

"Now!"

With that one word, Spike pulled the trigger on his gun and fired. His two brothers followed suit. The sounds of gunfire echoed throughout the wooded area. Several shots were unloaded upon the prone figure lying in front of them. The smell of gun smoke drifted through the air.

The barrage of gunfire the men unloaded upon Garrett was fearsome and deadly.

Within a few seconds it was over. Their gun barrels were still smoking, silent witnesses to the deadly deed the men had just done. Or at least it should have been deadly.

"Something's wrong." Spike said plainly.

The three men stared at their handiwork. The empty looks in their eyes seemed to only confirm what their older brother had just said. The sheets had been perforated with holes, but that was just about it. There was no blood gushing from where they had shot Garrett. There were no limbs from a corpse dangling awkwardly after having been shot through with lead. There was not even a single cry of pain from Garrett after they had shot him.

"What is this?"

Spike kicked away the sheets revealing a sack and some rocks positioned carefully together. The sheets and the hat had concealed the pile of rubbish enough to make it seem like a human sleeping on the ground. The three brothers stared at the empty pile and their eyes widened with shock.

"We've been had!"

"You bet your dirty hides you've been had all right!"

The three men turned and saw what seemed to be a pair of eyes staring right back at them from a nearby thicket.

The voice sounded old and weathered, but still very grim and dangerous. All three men immediately recognized who it was.

"Garrett! You there?" Spike said.

"You bet your worthless hide I am, Spike! An' I wouldn't recommend any of you moving. Y'all spent most of your lead on that pile of garbage there. Me? I got a full chamber of lead just waiting to rip y'all to shreds."

Despite Gruff's threats, Spike Dunlevy did not seem to be intimidated. The old marshal had turned the tables on their ambush, but he didn't seem concerned. He smiled and laughed right in the face of the imminent danger that was in front of them now. Perhaps he was merely trying to hide any feelings of fear and mounting panic.

"Haha! Is that so? Well, we ain't scared of ya! And it's still three of us, against one of you!" Spike said.

"You've got a lot of bluster for someone who just got the tables turned on 'em. This is yer last warning. I ain't going to repeat myself. Put your guns down and raise yer hands up in the air where I can see 'em!"

Spike looked around him. They still couldn't see where Gruff was exactly, but Spike could see his brothers. They didn't look as sure of themselves as he did. There was a look of clear desperation in both their faces. Even Bubba, who was usually confident and sure, looked confused and afraid now.

"What are we gonna do, Spike? I think Garrett has us dead to rights now!" Bubba said.

"Yeah, Spike. He cornered us an' faked us off with that sheet over all that junk! Maybe we should just..."

Devin hesitated to say it. Neither he nor Bubba wanted to upset Spike, even now. Neither of them could say it, but all three of them knew it. Gruff Garrett had gotten one over them again.

Spike's eyes lit up with a burning rage as the memory of the bank job flashed in his mind. This was exactly what had happened before, and it was happening all over again. Garrett had turned the tables on them, and had apprehended them, sending them to jail for those agonizing six months.

In a flash Spike remembered all the time spent behind those rusty bars of his cell. He remembered all the hours spent counting the time he and his brothers might have a chance of being free. The many hours of uncertainty and struggle to simply stay in the prison and endure.

When the time to break free from the prison came, Spike and his brothers jumped at the chance. In the riot, they almost died as well, but managed to escape. He remembered all those hard times, and in all of that, he never forgot the face of the man who put them all there. He never forgot about Gruff Garrett.

Spike remembered everything he and his brothers had endured for six months. Everything that had been set in motion when Garrett had apprehended him and his brothers. Spike remembered all that, and he could not bring himself to surrender to Garrett. Not again. Never again.

"You ain't takin' us lawdog! Not again! Fire at that bush boys!"

Spike turned towards the bush and pointed his gun there. His brothers saw what he was doing and followed as well. Gruff winced behind the bushes as he kept his pair of revolvers fixed on the brothers Dunlevy. He didn't want to do this, but he had no choice now. They had made their decision, and there was no turning back.

Gruff fired several shots from the bushes. Unlike the Dunlevy boys who had spent a lot of their ammo on a pile of garbage, Gruff still had two fresh cylinders worth of lead. Gruff fired several shots at the men in front of him, and all the bullets hit their mark.

Spike felt two shots rip through his chest as he went down. Bubba was hit by one shot right through his forehead, drilling right into his brain. Bubba was killed instantly, which was quite merciful. Devin was clipped on the arm, and he tried to fire back, but another shot struck him right above his nose and between his eyes. That bullet finished the job, and Devin fell, as well.

It was Spike who was on the ground and still barely alive. Spike was the only Dunlevy left. He looked up and saw Gruff Garrett walk towards him. Gruff now stood over him triumphantly. The old marshal looked down at the doomed outlaw, but there was no sense of pride or accomplishment in his eyes. There was only a look of deep regret. He shook his head and it was clear that he took no pride or joy from this victory.

"Damnation... you..."

Spike wanted to say something more. He struggled to spit out some more words, but his strength simply left him. Gruff pointed his gun towards Spike with the intent of finishing the job, with a shot to the head. He wouldn't have to. Spike expired without even completing whatever it was, he wanted to say.

"I didn't want to kill you boys, but you left me no choice. Why didn't you just drop your guns when I asked you to?" Gruff asked.

Silence was the only reply to Gruff's query. The

question hung in the air with no answer. There was no one left alive to answer his question. Gruff felt a slight breeze blow by, as if it were blowing his question away, unanswered.

The old lawdog felt something unusual hanging over him now. It was an unfamiliar and very heavy feeling that he did not like at all. Gruff felt a heavy burden on his heart and shoulders, something he had never felt before. When he had finished a job like this, there used to be a feeling of genuine pride and satisfaction at a job well done. This feeling of pride was there as recently as his last job taking down Ma Edgar and her murderous siblings. But now with the Dunlevys, Gruff did not feel any pride at all. He only felt very tired and a heavy sense of regret.

The painful memory of Katie Kemp flashed in Gruff's mind again. Everything changed when Katie took that bullet for him. In many ways, Katie wasn't the only good thing that died that die. On that day, his sense of pride and fulfilment in his work died too. On that day, it seemed as if Gruff truly felt old. He didn't just feel his age, he felt much older now. Gruff was now truly a tired old man with one last job to do.

Gruff took out an old shovel he thought he would never use. He began to dig up the dirt for a deep hole. It would be tedious work for Gruff, but he reckoned he could still manage despite his age. He even remembered something his doctor said about his heart needing some moderate exercise just to keep ticking. Well, digging a grave for these poor jerks was just the workout that Gruff needed.

Gruff found it surprising that he was even taking the time to dig a grave for these three men that had just tried to kill him earlier. It was definitely something of a radical change of heart. He could still remember a time when he would have just let their bodies rot and be food for carrion once. Perhaps Katie's death had affected him in a profound way.

"I guess I'm getting too old for this job, an' it's not just because I am old. Maybe it is the right time for me to retire all right. Maybe it would be right an' just if this would be my last job all right. Yeah. I just need to escort this prisoner, this John Bryan back to Chief Longsdale, and then I can do whatever it is that retired old lawdogs do." Gruff said to himself.

The thought of retirement now seemed more and more appealing for Gruff.

Chapter Three: The Mayor of Blue Rock

After burying the three outlaws, it didn't take long for Gruff to ride down to Blue Rock. Gruff hadn't heard much about this small town where the prisoner, a John Bryan was being kept. He also didn't know who this Monty Mathers was. He seemed like just another one of the many bounty hunters that were operating around the territories. The town itself didn't seem like any special town.

As he approached the town with Dynamite, his roan, Gruff was now eager to get this job done and to finally retire. The incident with the Dunlevy boys had definitely left a very sour taste in his mouth. After all these years Gruff was finally starting to feel the weight of being a US Marshal.

One might argue that the marshal was justified in taking down the Dunlevy brothers. A younger Gruff Garrett might have gotten much satisfaction for taking down another group of infamous outlaws, but he was not a young man, not anymore. There was nothing pleasant about killing those boys, even if they tried to ambush him. He felt no satisfaction taking them down, even if they refused to step down after his warning.

Garrett rode Dynamite into the small town. Nothing seemed out of the ordinary as he entered the small, sleepy town. He hitched Dynamite on a hitching pike, and started to walk around the town. Gruff figured the best way to find this Monty Mathers was to ask around town.

He didn't get far when he noticed a man lying on the ground in front of one of the town's establishments. Gruff dismissed the sight at first. After all, he had seen his fair share of drunks that had passed out in front of establishments. There were even some days that it was Gruff himself who had passed out like that. Upon closer examination of the prone man however, Gruff discovered something quite not right.

Gruff moved closer towards the man. He saw that he was not moving. Perhaps he was deep in slumber.

"Hey, mister! Best you get up lest you catch something out here." he said.

Gruff tried to nudge the man awake. After all, it

wouldn't be pleasant at all to spend the night alone in the street like this in a drunk stupor. Gruff had experienced this before, so many years ago. He wouldn't want someone else to go through it, if he could help it.

"Come on, mister. Get up. I'll help you get a room or something where you can spend the night."

The man didn't respond, and Gruff tried to nudge him a little harder. Perhaps he was just really drunk. Gruff got close enough to see that the man wasn't drunk at all. The blood from a gunshot wound to the head confirmed that he was dead.

"Good Lord! He's a goner!" Gruff said.

"Surprised? That poor galoot's been dead since yesterday when the mayor shot his lights out!"

Gruff looked up and saw a young lady calling to him. The lady smiled at him with an inviting smile.

"The mayor shot him?" Gruff asked.

"Yep. Sure did. You sound surprised about that. I think you're not from these parts are you, old timer? Why don't you come up here with me? Maybe you need to relax after a long and weary journey. Come on. I can make it worth your while. I'll even give you a discount."

"Lady, you don't know how tempting your offer is right now. I would gladly take you up on it, if I wasn't busy with some matters to attend to."

"Really now? Well, too bad! If ever you decide to change your mind, you know where to find me. I'm Cassie Kendrick by the way."

She was young and attractive and had a voice that sounded like a nightingale or any other singing bird. She seemed quite innocent, but one look and Gruff knew that she was anything but. The young girl exuded an air of innocence despite working in a shady establishment like this. Gruff looked up at her, and he realized that she reminded him of Katie Kemp. Just like Katie, she was very pretty with an air of fresh innocence, despite her line of work. Even her name sounded similar to Katie's in some way.

"Gruff Garrett, and I'm pleased to make your acquaintance there, Casey. Know where I might find the mayor of your little town?"

"All right. You don't know where Mayor Mathers is? You're really not from here, all right."

When he heard the name of the mayor, Gruff's ears almost went up like a dog that heard the dinner bell. His name definitely rang a bell or three.

"Mayor Mathers you say? Mayor Monty Mathers?"

"Yep. That's Hizzoner's name all right. The great Mayor of our small an' humble lil' mining town here."

Marshal Garrett had been well-traveled and had seen his fair share of towns around several counties and territories. Despite this, he was not familiar with Blue Rock and for good reason. Small mining towns like it, often sprang up when gold was discovered nearby. Once the gold rush ended, such towns often were abandoned as well. This would probably be the fate of Blue Rock.

It was no wonder that they would elect a mayor like the bounty hunter Monty Mathers. Such small towns often enforced their own laws and regulations. Out here in the middle of nowhere, such laws were quite flexible, and small mining towns like this were often a trouble magnet. These were the places where you would find drifters running away from some kind of past, or outlaws running from the law. Garrett wasn't familiar with the small town, but he was very familiar with the things happening around in it.

"Looks like your mayor's a man of many talents." Gruff said.

Casey smiled. "Oh, he definitely is! If you're looking for him, you're on the right track. Just keep going straight then take the second road to the right. You'll find the mayor's office right there. Can't miss it." she said.

"Straight then second road to the right. Simple enough directions. I'll be going there then. Thanks for the directions, Casey."

Gruff turned and walked away nonchalantly. After the cordial discussion with Casey, it didn't seem to matter too much that a dead man was lying on the street. Gruff was used to seeing such things anyway, and the important thing was that he was pointed in the right direction to Monty Mathers.

Casey had given Garrett clear enough directions to find Mathers' office, but he wouldn't need them. There were more than enough indicators to lead him to Mathers' place. For one thing, there was an office at the end of the street that Casey had directed Gruff to. The office looked old and run down with fading paint, and cracked windows. The wooden door at the front of the office looked like it was about to fall off. There was no mistaking that it had to be Mathers' establishment. The large sign that was tacked on the old office was indication enough. It was a wooden sign with the words "Mayor's Office" painted on it.

Gruff approached the old office and was surprised when he heard the sounds of shrieking and cries of agony inside. It sounded like someone was being tortured in the old office.

"What in tarnation is going on in there?" Gruff thought to himself.

He cautiously opened the unlocked door of the mayor's office, not sure what to expect. The shrieks and screams of agony were coming from another room in the small office. There was another man who sat calmly in the waiting area of the office. The man seemed oblivious to what was going on in the other room.

"Excuse me, Sir. I'm looking for uh, Monty Mathers. And uh... do you know what's going on inside there?" Gruff said.

"If you're looking for Monty Mathers, well, you've come to the right place. This is his office all right. And you sound surprised at what's happening? Didn't you come here to get one of your teeth extracted?" the man said.

"Teeth extracted? Monty's a dentist too?" Gruff asked.

The man nodded. "Yes sir. He's the only dentist round these parts."

Gruff couldn't believe what he was hearing. Looks like Casey knew what she was talking about, all right. When she said Monty was a man of many talents, she was definitely right. He was not just a bounty hunter, he was also the mayor of this small backwater town, and its only dentist. The man was a veritable Jack of All Trades.

"So, you didn't come here to get your teeth extracted?" the man asked again.

Gruff shook his head. "Nope. I'm here for official business. So I don't need to wait in line now, do I?"

The man said something again, but Gruff ignored him and marched straight into the next room. Gruff saw one man hunched over another man that was sitting on a

reclined chair. The standing man was using what appeared to be rusty implements as the other man opened his mouth wide. The sitting man also appeared to be squirming and in great pain now. This whole strange tableau did not seem to bother Gruff in the least bit.

"Awright, Monty Moses, was it?" Gruff said.

The standing man turned towards Gruff with a stinky look in his eye. He appeared to be of middle age, with a thick beard and a fairly large frame.

"It's Monty Mathers, and get back in line! Can't you see I'm in the middle of a delicate procedure here?" he said.

"Monty Mathers yeah, sorry. I mix up them names once in a while. Must come with age, eh? Well, I didn't come here to get a tooth extracted. I came here on official business for the US government. I heard you've got a prisoner here, John Bryan. Well, I'm a deputized US Marshal an' I'm here to collect the prisoner."

Upon hearing Gruff's business here, Monty Mathers gave him a strange look. It was a look of annoyance mixed with genuine relief. It was a strange look that Gruff couldn't really understand.

"So you're the one they sent to take that rotten prisoner out of here? Great! I'll be more than happy to surrender him to yer custody and claim my reward for him. Just gimme a sec here. As you can see, this is delicate work you're interrupting!"

"My apologies, sir! I'll just wait on out at the back."

Gruff went back to the waiting area and sat down. Monty took his time extracting the poor man's tooth. It was just as he said. Such delicate and agonizing work took time, and couldn't be rushed. Gruff fell in and out of consciousness as he sat there, waiting for Mathers to finish. He winked off to the sound of the other man's cries of pain and agony.

Gruff was just having a fairly vague but pleasant dream, when he was rudely roused from his slumber. He woke up to the sound of howls of protest.

"Aaahhh! Stay away from me!"

Gruff opened his eyes and saw the man that had been sitting in the dentist's chair. He was standing up now and had rushed out of the other room. The poor man was clutching his bleeding mouth with one hand. There was a look of sheer terror in his eyes.

"Come on now, Bill! It's all over now. I got the tooth out, didn't I?" Mathers said.

Mathers looked quite calm and unapologetic, despite Bill's clearly terrified look.

"Yeah! You sure did get the tooth out, after nearly killing me!"

Mathers nonchalantly shrugged his shoulders. "Hey, I did what I could with the tools available! Far as I know, that's the only way to extract a tooth! Unless you want to go to the big cities and try them fancy doctors there. If you got the money, go for it!"

"If I did have some cash on me, that's exactly what I would have done!" the man said.

"Oh, don't be such a crybaby! The tooth's been extracted. That's what's important! Just keep pressin' on that wound there where I pulled it off, an' the bleeding and the pain will stop. Eventually."

The man didn't bother to try and argue anymore. He couldn't see the point of it all. He just walked away, leaving Monty where he stood.

"Ah, now that was a rather unpleasant bit of business there. Unfortunately, it just couldn't be avoided. Anyway, I'll deal with you first Marshal. After that, I can resume with your tooth extraction, eh? After all, the marshal and I have some official business to settle first."

Mathers turned to the man who was sitting at the waiting area. He had seen the whole thing go down with the man whose tooth had just been pulled out. He was starting to sweat nervously on his forehead. He turned to Mathers and shook his head.

"You know, I thought my tooth was aching earlier, but on second thought, I think I'll just pass on the tooth extraction, for now."

"What? You're beggin' off? Come on! Don't worry

about it. Old Joe Wagner there was always something of a yellow belly. Don't let what happened to him get to you. I'll have that tooth out before you know it."

The man was not convinced with Mathers' words of encouragement. No words of encouragement could erase what he had just seen earlier. The man promptly stood up and left Mathers' office.

"Ah, fine! Suit yourself! Less work for me today! I wasn't in the mood to pull another tooth anyway!"

"Sorry about your customers, but I'm here to take the prisoner out of your hands." Gruff said.

"That you are. Come on. I'll take you to him."

Monty led Garrett out to the back of his office. They came upon another small and dilapidated structure. Garrett saw that there was also a wooden sign that was hung over the front door. The words 'jailhouse' was crudely painted on the sign.

Gruff chuckled. It seemed Mathers liked to keep everything in order. Or at least he tried to keep everything in order.

"He's right in here. I'm only too eager to get rid of him." Mathers said.

"I can see the prisoner's been giving you a headache."

Mathers rolled his eyes and shook his head. "Headache, eh? Well that's putting it up mildly."

"He that much trouble to you?" Gruff asked.

Mathers smiled and shook his head. "The rascal won't stop yapping and blabbering about how he ain't being treated right and how his gang's coming to spring him. I would love that you take him just so I can have some peace an' quiet for once."

"I heard that! An' I ain't lying when I say my boys are coming to spring me outta here! When they come here after me, you're a dead man Mathers! A dead man!"

Mathers did not seem the least bit affected by the prisoner's rantings. He only seemed annoyed.

"What did I tell you? Ain't no way to shut that man's trap."

Garrett heard the prisoner all right, and there was something familiar about his voice. Garrett was sure that he had heard that voice before. He was just not sure when or where. When Garrett and Mathers walked towards the prisoner, he couldn't believe what or who he was seeing. He knew the voice was familiar, but he never expected to see this man here.

"Well, I'll be. Paolo 'Poison' Dixon!"

Garrett stared at the dark-skinned man with the long black hair that was tied up in strange curls in front of him. His well-built muscular frame was exposed and highlighted by torn clothing. Garrett could still remember Dixon by his devotion to his ethnic dance and culture, how he would play a strange tune with his gang the "Poison Club", in the middle of a gunfight. When Dixon spoke to him, Garrett knew it was his old enemy who was standing in front of him again.

"Garrett? Is that you? I always thought it was going to be your last jogo all those years Garrett man. Somehow, you've managed to survive to be an old man! Hahaha!"

"I can't believe I would bump into you here, Dixon. I can still remember you dancing around like a fool in those old barfights."

Dixon grinned at Garrett from behind the rusty bars.

"That is Capoeira, my country's fighting style. The style that was banned by our colonial masters, but still survives to this day. The art that was taught to me by my master before I traveled to this new and hostile country."

Garrett shook his head. "I'm not impressed. If you ask me, you just looked like a headless chicken dancing around without its head."

Dixon laughed maniacally. "Say what you want about it, but I still remember all the times my boot landed in your face. How you still somehow manage to have a full set of chompers at your age is beyond me."

"I'm a lot tougher than you or anyone else give me credit for, Dixon."

"You two know each other?"

Mathers sounded shocked and surprised that Garrett knew the prisoner. From the way they were talking they seemed to have a long and bitter history dating back many years ago.

"Know each other? Heh! Me an' Garrett there go way back! Really way back!" Dixon said.

"I hate to admit it but yes, we do have a sick and twisted history that goes well… yes. Way back."

"Ain't that something? So this dirtbag ain't even using his real name?" Mathers asked.

"No! I don't know where he got the idea of using John Bryan, but his real name's Paolo Dixon. He's from some other region where they practice that dancing, fighting art form or whatever they call it. Not really sure, but along the way, Dixon learned how to draw a gun aside from just prancing around. Made him a lot more deadly too. And that gang of his? The Poison Club? I've dealt with them before. I'm not sure just how loyal they are to this man, but they are pretty deadly indeed."

"A lot more deadly n' you two will ever be!" Dixon boasted.

"Well, whatever the case may be, let 'em come. I'm not afraid of them at all. I think you may have passed by my own handiwork on the way here." Mathers said.

"If you mean the dead man on the street? Yeah, yeah,

I saw him all right. I thought he was sleeping, but this nice, young lady told me otherwise." Gruff said.

"That was Charles Coburn. Been stirring up trouble for a while here. I tried to reason with 'em but well, he drew a gun on me, and I guess I had to do, what I had to do."

"Ain't no doubt that you can handle yourself here, Mathers. I reckon that means I can take this dirtbag off of your hands."

"He's all yours, Garrett. Just feed him here first. There's some slop I made. It should be enough to keep him full. I may not like him, but I'm not one to let a man go to prison on an empty stomach. That's just not me. You can take him by the dawn's early light tomorrow. Me? I think I heard another customer come for a tooth extraction. I'll get to that first."

Mathers stepped out of the jailhouse and back to his dental office leaving Garrett alone with Dixon. The two old rivals were alone now, separated only by the rusty bars that held Dixon back. If it were up to the old lawdog, he would have loved to plug Dixon right here.

They did have a long history that would have probably justified it. But of course, that was not how Dixon was. After all, if he did that he wouldn't be living up to his ideals as a marshal. It was just really difficult to keep his emotions in check, as he never expected to be escorting his old rival Paolo Dixon back to the marshals.

"Guess I'm going to have to shovel some slop on you right now." Garrett said.

Dixon sneered at his old rival. "Oh you shovel it down good, Marshal. You wouldn't want me to go with you on that long trip back to the marshals on an empty stomach now, would you?"

Garrett shook his head. "If it were up to me Dixon, I would let you starve. Or put a bullet through your head, right now. After everything you've done, and everything that's come between us, God knows you deserve as much. But that ain't how I want to be remembered as a marshal."

"So this was supposed to be your last job, eh? To escort me out of here and back into custody? For a proper trial and such? Heh. Guess you didn't expect me to be the prisoner you were escorting. And the years have not been kind to ya! Heheh!"

"You ain't no spring chicken yourself, Dixon. Shut up."

Garrett walked towards a soup bowl that was placed on a table. The soup was hot and Garrett could smell the aroma. It was actually a little appetizing. He wondered if cooking was another talent that you could chalk up to Monty Mathers. Garrett actually found that quite amazing. Mathers seemed like a very talented individual, someone who was a lot more than what he seemed. It would be a shame if Mathers were gunned down by the Poison Club. But that would also be assuming that Dixon was telling the truth and that they were coming for him. Garrett couldn't really be sure if Dixon were telling the truth. In all the time they had tangled, Garrett couldn't say that Dixon was a straight shooter. If anything, he was an outlaw, and an outlaw's word wasn't worth much. He may have been bluffing and the entire thing about his gang coming for him, might be an empty threat. Even if he led the gang, there was no real way to tell just how loyal they were to him. And even if they did come after him and tangle with Mathers, Mathers looked like a very capable individual. From what Garrett had seen so far, Mathers looked every bit the deadly bounty hunter who could take care of himself. And besides none of that really mattered now. The only thing that mattered for Garrett was to bring Dixon in and finish his last job.

"This slop actually smells good. Too good for someone like you." Garrett said, as he scooped some of the soup into a bowl.

"Heh. Just get me something to eat already."

Garrett was just about to hand the hot bowl of slop over to Dixon when Mathers came back into the jailhouse. The two men turned towards him, surprised that he came back so soon.

"That was quick. I reckon nobody pulls out a tooth that fast without some serious consequences." Garrett said.

Mathers nodded. "Yeah, exactly. That's because the men outside aren't here to get their teeth pulled out." he said.

"What? What are you saying?" Gruff said.

Mathers turned to Dixon. "Looks like you're a lot more popular than anyone gave you credit for Dixon. The men are here to get to you too."

65

Chapter Four: They'll Kill You

The three men barged into the jailhouse, just after Mathers spoke. The men had large, muscular frames that were still prominent, despite the furs they wore. The men also sported thick beards and were armed with guns that were worn with constant use. Gruff didn't know who these men were, but it was clear at first glance that they were fur trappers. Mountain men like these were a hardy sort, living off of the land constantly dealing with Indians, settlers, wild animals and anything in between. Men like these were used to any kind of conflict and messing with them was never a good idea.

Gruff had no idea who these men were but upon seeing them, Dixon smiled gleefully from behind his rusty cell.

"Been a while Dawson. You still runnin' with your boys there, man?"

One of the mountain men sneered right back at Dixon, revealing rows of yellow teeth, with some missing. He wore a beaver hat that seemed to only make his scowl even more menacing.

"Of course. Unlike you Cray, me an' the boys value loyalty." Dawson said.

"Yeah. We stick together to the end. Something a back stabbing snake like yourself would struggle to understand."

"Cray? That another alias of yours, Dixon? I thought it was John Bryan. Now it's 'Cray'. You never introduced yerself with your real name ever, did you?" Garrett said.

Dixon smiled gleefully as he shook his head. "Of course not! You know me. I'm a very private person. Only a few people like you, ever knew the real me."

"We're not surprised you used different aliases. A snake like you can't ever be counted on to tell the truth. So now me an' the boys are going to take you down once and for all."

It was Fig Brewster who spoke. Brewster had a booming voice just like Dan Dawson, with a physique

that was just as imposing. Their silent companion

was of mixed descent, like Paolo Dixon. Unlike the other two, the half-breed Indian did not speak, but the hatred in his eyes for Paolo Dixon was unmistakable. It was the same look of pure hatred that was reflected in Dan Dawson and Fig Brewster's eyes. These men were here for only one goal, and that was to kill Paolo Dixon.

Dixon himself, remained quite unaffected. He brushed off the men's threats and continued to smile defiantly. "Me, a backstabbing snake? Heh. You hurt my feelings, Fig my man. I would like to think that I'm more of a practical sort, than a backstabber."

"We'll do more than just hurt your feelings you piece of filth! We'll make sure you ain't gonna hurt no more. Permanently."

"Now that you boys put it as such, I'm assuming you want to take the prisoner, don't you?" Mathers said.

Dawson nodded grimly. "That's right. We're here to take that no good owl-hoot off of your hands and make sure he don't hurt nobody, no more. Not now or ever."

Mathers whistled low. Gruff was about to say something, but it was Mathers who spoke first.

"Well, if that's the case we've got something of a problem. You see, I did collar that "piece of filth" as you boys so succinctly put it, for the reward on his head. The marshal here is set to pay me and..."

Fig Brewster raised a hand and interrupted Mathers. "We're well aware of what Dixon's worth, and we're prepared to pay double to take him.

Mathers' eyes lit up, and the expression on his face drastically changed. It was only moments earlier that he was about to strongly protest these men taking Dixon. Now, he sang a different, and more accommodating tone.

"Well, now that you put it that way, I'm not going to protest. He's all yours." Mathers said.

"Hold on a minute, there! Ain't no one taking that prisoner but me! I was sent here by the US Marshals to take that man into custody and by golly, that's what I'm going to do!" Gruff said.

Dawson shook his head as he looked Gruff straight in the eye. "Don't do it, Marshal. That prisoner is lower than a snake crawling the lowest level of hell, an' you know it! You're old and you don't need to get into any kind of trouble on his behalf!" Dawson said.

Gruff shook his head, and was just as firm and steadfast with his words. A part of him was surprised and almost shocked to hear him speak like this.

"I may be old, but I'm more than capable to do my job. And my job is to take this prisoner with me back to the US Marshals!"

"I can't believe you're all fighting over little old me! Hahaha, this is just hilarious. It would even be more hilarious if it wasn't my neck on the line!" Dixon said.

"Shut your pie hole Dixon, before I change my mind! I can't believe I'm actually trying to stick my neck out for you, of all people!"

"Listen to Dan, Marshal. There's three of us, and just one of you. An old timer like yourself wouldn't want to get into all this trouble for a lowlife like Dixon!" Brewster said.

For a moment, Gruff Garrett pondered the mountain man's words. There was definitely sense to what he said. They were three young mountain men at the peak of their youth and heath. Garrett was an aging gunslinger on his last job. If he were younger, he would have probably even relished taking on these three mountain men. The risk and danger wouldn't matter, as youth tended to blind many men and make them reckless.

Garrett knew this fact, all too well. It was because of this, that he wasn't as eager to get into skirmishes like this, as he used to. Even before he got into this mess, Garrett was already starting to lose his enthusiasm for his whole job. Garrett was starting to see less of the idealism in upholding the law, and more of the risky nature of the job, along with the constant death. He was already starting to re-evaluate everything because of Katie Kemp's death. He didn't need to get into something like this again.

Despite his misgivings, Garrett realized that he still had a job to do. He had signed up to bring this prisoner back to his superiors, and that was just what he intended to do. It didn't matter if he didn't know that the prisoner was his old rival Paolo Dixon. It didn't matter that he was now facing danger that he probably wasn't prepared for. All of that really didn't matter for a grizzled old lawdog like Gruff Garrett. What mattered most to him was getting the job done, no matter what.

"I got a job to do boys, and I intend to do it, no matter what you think!"

The three mountain men looked at each other. They shared a look that was equal parts disappointment, regret, and grit. They shot that look right back at Gruff and held their ground.

"We're really sorry to hear that old timer. We came here for Dixon, not for you. But if you insist on being such a stickler for the law well, it's three of us, and just one of you." Dawson said.

"Three of you, one of me. I've handled worse." Gruff said.

He spoke plainly and with much grit. Gruff did his best to hide the growing tension and fear inside of him. After all, Dawson was right. It was three against one, and he was an old man. This wasn't going to be easy but Gruff had made his choice, and so had the mountain men. There was no turning back from either side now.

"Well, seeing as you four ain't going to talk about this, I better get moving. I sure don't want to get caught in the crossfire or something like that." Mathers said.

"Mathers, you're a coward! You ain't going to help Gruff or something? You can't just up an' leave!" Dixon said.

Dixon spoke with tension and growing fear in his voice. This seemed to be the first time that he ever betrayed any hint of fear, since this all started.

"I sure can do whatever I want! As far as I'm concerned, this ain't none of my business! The only thing that matters is getting rid of you and making some kind of profit out of it!"

"You slimy rat! Get back in here!" Dixon said.

It was no use. Mathers had turned his back on all of them and was already walking out of the jailhouse. Garrett wasn't really surprised at Mathers' decision to walk out. He was clearly a practical man, and there was no practical sense in taking a side here. It was much better for him to sort everything out once this was all over. Garrett hoped that when the smoke cleared, he would be the one left standing. That of course, was not a guarantee. Nothing ever was in this line of work.

The mountain men were hardier and younger, that was for sure. Gruff was no match for them in a physical fight. But the old lawdog had something more going for him, and that were his experience and instincts. One complemented the other, and in the whole time they had been standing there, Gruff hadn't just been chatting with them. He had been sizing them up. While they had been talking, Gruff had never let his gaze wander. His eyes had been focused solely on the three mountain men in front of him. Every sense he had was trained and focused on the three men, ready to spring into action at the slightest provocation.

When Fig Brewster reached for the shotgun on his hip, Gruff was quick to notice it. He may have been old but his senses were still razor sharp. He noticed the slightest hint of Brewster shifting his weight and moving his arm. Gruff knew that he was going for his shotgun and it was time to act.

Gruff didn't even think anymore and simply let his instincts take over. He drew his revolver and fired at whatever was moving in front of him. Gruff unloaded a barrage of lead before the mountain men could even react. He unloaded five shots. Two missed the mark completely, but the other three were right on the spot.

Brewster and Dawson crumpled to the ground. Both men clutched their guts as they fell. Neither managed to pull off a single shot. Brewster managed to mumble a few words before oblivion swallowed him up.

"That was fast... for an... old timer..."

Garrett had struck them all with his shooting, but the half-breed Indian was still standing. He was even tougher and hardier than his two companions. He had taken a bullet to the side of his stomach. The man was wincing in pain, and the blood was gushing from where the bullet had torn into him. Garrett knew that such a shot was fatal, but the mountain didn't seem to know that. Either that, or he was determined to take Garrett down to hell with him. Either way, the man was still standing.

"Them Blackfoot are a hardy sort! Take 'em down Gruff! Take 'em down!"

From behind his cell, Dixon cheered Garrett on. The old lawdog did not appreciate the words of encouragement at all.

"Shut yer trap, Dixon! I'm not doing this for you!"

The large mountain man lunged at Garrett. It was all Garrett could do to avoid the lunge. The large man was shockingly fast, despite his large size and his gunshot wound. Garrett barely dodged the lunge, relying on his own unusual burst of speed borne from the moment of desperation. The large mountain man slammed onto the rusty bars in front of Dixon, rattling and shaking his cell, as he did so. Dixon pulled back. He caught a glimpse of the mountain man's face as he did so. Their eyes met and Dixon trembled as he saw nothing but hate and pain in his face.

The mountain man eyed Gruff from where he was standing. They were only standing some distance apart. Gruff could feel his old ticker pounding now, as the tension in the small jailhouse was palpable.

"I'm getting too old for this sort of thing!" Gruff said.

He still had one shot left in his chamber before he needed to reload. It was an enclosed space, and the mountain man wasn't far from Gruff. It should have been an easy shot, but between his pounding ticker and the angry mountain man rushing him, Gruff just couldn't get a good shot off. He fired and the shot missed wildly, piercing a hole through the jailhouse's old wall.

The mountain man came rushing at Gruff who could not avoid him now. He raised a knee instinctively, hoping that the mountain man would run into it, and hopefully stun him. Normally, a low blow like that would be enough to knock the wind out of any man but this was a different situation entirely. The mountain man was bleeding from the side of his stomach. It was a potentially fatal wound, but adrenalin and the rush of pure rage was now fueling him. He wasn't stopping for a bullet wound. A low blow was now simply just par for the course.

The mountain man plowed through Gruff's knee and knocked him down as he rushed him. Gruff thought that he twisted his knee. It might ache but he would probably manage. At his age, he was used to all sorts of aches and pains all over his body. A bum knee would be very manageable that is, if he even survived this encounter.

The mountain man knocked Gruff to the ground, and

was now on top of him. They rolled and struggled around in the ground for a while, but eventually, the mountain man managed to get right back on top of him. It was not a very ideal position for Gruff to be in.

Gruff felt one punch, then another and then another. The punches were heavy and felt like metal sledgehammers raining down upon his head. The pain was intense, but Gruff forced himself to focus. Through the haze of pain and agony, he saw something that might be his salvation. It was a knife lying on the floor. It must have been owned by one of the other mountain men. Now, if Gruff could reach it, it could actually save Gruff's life.

He stretched and reached for the knife. The mountain man was so focused on pummeling Gruff and blocking out his own pain from the gunshot wound, that he never noticed him reaching for the knife. Once Gruff got ahold of the knife, he acted swiftly and without hesitation. Gruff gripped the knife and drove it straight behind the mountain man's skull. Gruff didn't even struggle as he drove the knife to the back of the man's head. Somehow, he had managed to catch the mountain man off-guard with one swift stretch and jab. The mountain man's eyes widened with pain and shock as the knife was dug right behind his head. He couldn't believe what was happening, but there was no way to stop it now.

Gruff felt the knife penetrate the soft part of the man's head, and he kept stabbing and stabbing repeatedly. Gruff kept stabbing at the man until all expression in his eyes and face had left him. There was nothing but a blank expression on his face that was devoid of life and awareness. The light of life had left the man, but Gruff kept stabbing. He still kept stabbing even as the man fell forward on top of him. Gruff was already drenched in the man's own blood from the back of his head, but he couldn't stop stabbing.

"Stop! Gruff! Stop it already! He's dead! You killed him already. It's over!"

It was Dixon. Gruff heard Dixon's voice, and the sound of it roused him from the temporary madness that had taken over him. Gruff had been snapped back into reality. He realized now that Dixon was right. It was over, and there was no point in stabbing the back of the dead man's head over and over.

Gruff dropped the knife and took a deep breath. He gathered his strength and with much effort, turned the dead man over so he could get up from the ground. It took Gruff a lot of effort, but somehow, he managed to get the dead man's corpse off of him. Gruff managed to get up. His arms and legs were shaking, clearly from the shock of what had just happened. Now that the danger had passed, Gruff also felt his ticker beating off of his chest. He knew that this kind of tension wasn't good for him, and he hastily dug into his shirt pocket for another of his heart starter pills. Gruff popped it into his mouth and slowly, his ticker began to beat more steadily and less frantically.

"Good Lord above. You're taking nitro pills?" Dixon said.

"They're for my heart, Dixon! I ain't as young as I used to be." Gruff said, as he clutched at his chest.

The tightening in his chest was slowly but surely loosening now. The danger of an imminent heart attack had passed again. Gruff was relieved that he survived again, but he didn't know how long he could keep this up. The next time he suffered another potential heart attack could be the last one. He didn't know just how long he could keep pushing his luck.

"I can't believe you actually managed to take them all out like that. Gotta say, I didn't think you had it in you, Garrett! For an old timer, you've still got a lot of kick left in you!"

Garrett leaned on the wall to steady his shaky legs. Even he couldn't believe that he got out of that scrape alive.

"Shut up, Dixon. This ain't no game. I just got a job to do, and I aim to do it, no matter what."

"Heh. You got a lot of grit and fortitude for an old timer, Garrett. I'll give you that much. But even all that ain't going to be enough when my boys come lookin' for me. You take me away, I guarantee they're going to come lookin' for me, an' they'll follow us to the ends of the earth."

Dixon stared right into Garrett's eyes, boring a hole right through them.

"They're going to kill you to get to me, Garrett. I promise you that."

Garrett appeared unfazed by Dixon's warning. He didn't seem to take the threat of his gang coming for him very seriously. He was just relieved to have survived this far.

"Whatever. Get some rest, Dixon. We'll leave at the first signs of the early dawn light tomorrow. I will get you back to the marshals no matter what."

Chapter Five: High and Mighty

When the excitement had died down, Gruff led his roan Dynamite to the nearby livery barn, he had spied in the small mining town. He noticed no one seemed particularly alarmed or concerned that shots had been fired in the mayor's jailhouse. Gruff wasn't really surprised that the people were so nonchalant. Miners were usually a tough and hardy lot. You needed to be, if you were to work in such perilous conditions like an underground cave, prospecting for gold. A few shots here and there wouldn't really matter much to men like that.

The liveryman was a black man by the name of Henry Leaden. Leaden wasn't as old as Gruff, but his tired eyes betrayed a man who had seen much more than his years.

"Take good care of my roan, mister. That's my ride outta this little town of yours." Gruff said.

Leaden gently patted and stroked the side of Dynamite's neck. His casual gestures showed that he was experienced in dealing with horses.

"Don't worry Marshal. He'll be safe here until the

morning when you'll need him. I suggest you get some shuteye at the tent shack just across from here. The cots are pretty comfortable, all things considered."

Gruff nodded and tipped his hat. "I'll take that advice of yours. Thanks, Mister. I'll get Dynamite early tomorrow morning before the dawn's light breaks."

Leaden nodded, and Gruff calmly walked in the direction of the tent shack. It was a short walk through the small mining town.

Gruff passed by a man who appeared to be walking on shaky legs. The man seemed to struggle to keep his balance, as his legs shook and he teetered and trembled. Finally, the man fell to the ground with a soft thud.

At first, Gruff thought that the man was a drunk who had too much to drink. It wasn't uncommon to find men stumbling over their own feet in mining towns like this. The men were often under a lot of stress and drinking more than their fair share of alcohol was to be expected, sometimes. Gruff glanced at the man for a half-second longer and realized that he wasn't just another drunk who had a really bad hangover. The handle of a knife in his back along with some of its exposed blade proved as much. The man had been stabbed.

A man and a woman were passing by as well and giggling like little kids. It was clear they both had gotten too much to drink, as well. They saw the man lying on the ground with the exposed blade protruding from his back. They both gave him a quick glance and moved on their merry way.

"This is a rough little mining town, ain't it?" Gruff said.

Another man ambled towards the dead man's corpse and pulled out the bloody knife. He did it quickly enough, and showed some concern that he was doing it out in the open, however, it didn't seem to be enough to discourage him.

For a moment, the two men's eyes met, but it was Gruff who looked away. There was no point in even trying to uphold law and order around here. Even if Gruff wanted to do something, this little town wasn't in his jurisdiction anyway. Gruff wasn't about to risk his neck unnecessarily. He had already accepted a good amount of risk taking this job, and still deciding to see it through when he realized it was his old rival Paolo Dixon he was fetching. For a moment, Gruff wondered if the wily outlaw was indeed telling the truth about his gang coming after him. Were they really trying to find and rescue him? If so, that would mean even more trouble for Gruff. That wasn't something he was looking forward to, if ever it was true. With Paolo Dixon, Gruff couldn't really be sure about anything. This job was turning out to be a lot more complicated than he expected or wanted it to be.

When Gruff arrived at the tent shack, he promptly paid for a cot. He had to duck a little under the covers of the tent, as it wasn't that high. Gruff wasn't a short man, but he wasn't that tall either.

A round black man took his money and was managing the tent shack. He resembled the liveryman, and Gruff could only assume they might be brothers.

"I was directed here by the liveryman across the street. I just need a cot to sleep and some grub for the night."

"Yeah. That would be my brother Isaac. He runs the livery stable round here. Don't worry mister. He's pretty good with them horses. The man whispers things in their ears. The kind of things them animals want to hear. I'm Bart, by the way. I run this little tent shack for weary travelers who want to rest up and get some grub. I can also prepare you a good meal of pork strips and some hot chocolate with some biscuits if you would like."

Gruff was more than a little famished from the encounter with the three mountain men earlier. The prospect of getting a hot meal out here sounded very appetizing indeed.

"Yeah, I would like that. Thank you very much, Bart."

"You just sit tight there Mister? I'll prepare your meal in a bit."

"It's Garrett. Gruff Garrett, US Marshal."

"Well, don't you worry Marshal sir. I'll prepare your meal to give you a little pick me up so you can keep upholding the law."

Bart directed him to one of the three long tables in

the tent. From across Gruff there were two other old men sitting and chatting. They looked to be just a little younger than Gruff, which wasn't much.

The two old men looked just as grizzled and ornery as Gruff was. He paid them no heed, and soon enough his thoughts were drifting back to when this whole crazy job started. He suddenly remembered the terrible image of Katie Kemp bleeding out in the middle of the street. He could still remember how terrible he felt. How her death felt so heavy and senseless, and how Gruff had somehow let the young and pretty lady in waiting down. Her death still weighed heavily on Gruff's conscience, even if he wasn't the man who had pulled the trigger. The fact that the bullet was meant for him was enough for it to weigh heavily upon him.

"Katie, Katie. What a waste. What a terrible waste that you had to die like that. I should have protected you. I should have saved you."

Not even the arrival of his meal was enough to cheer up

Gruff. He took one bite of the pork strips and he

realized that Bart was a pretty good cook. The hot chocolate tasted very well, and the aroma was very inviting. It was all well-prepared, but Gruff still couldn't get Katie out of his mind. Something like that wasn't going to be drowned out by just one good meal.

"Katie, Katie. You died too young and on my account. How am I ever going to set things right?"

"Set what things right, Mister Marshal there?"

Gruff turned and saw that one of the old men was talking to him. His tone and choice of words were clearly disrespectful.

"It's nothing. It don't concern you. I was just talkin' to myself." Gruff said.

"I dunno. From where I'm sittin' it sure seemed like you was disrespecting' me. Sayin' I gotta set things right an' square."

The old man leaned closer to Gruff. Gruff could smell the scent of whiskey on the old timer. He also noticed that the old man spoke in a slurred manner. The signs were all there. He had drunk a whole lot of whiskey. Too much whiskey, and it was causing him to speak and act just a little too impulsively.

Gruff raised a hand. "Mister, you've had too much to drink. I ain't here to cause no trouble. I'm a US Marshal here on official business and…"

"Oh, so you think that you're someone all high and mighty, eh? You think you're some kind of a bigshot who can just come in here wavin' his badge like that actin' like you're king of the hill or something?"

The old man was clearly agitated now, but for no good reason. Gruff didn't want to provoke him. He wanted to quickly de-escalate the situation. After his run-in with those mountain men earlier, Gruff was in no mood to tackle another rough customer.

"You better take it easy, Mister. You've clearly had too much to drink and you're talkin' nonsense. I could take you in now for threatening an officer of the law, but I'm inclined to show leniency considering that it's been a long day for me. Now, I'm not going to say this again. Take it easy and just step back. I ain't here to cause no trouble with you or anyone. I just want to eat my grub in peace and get some shuteye later."

"Take it easy Hawk. The marshal just wants to eat in peace. He ain't in no mood to start nuthin'. If you ask me, you're outta line and you should be thankful that he's in a generous mood. I would back off now, while you still had a chance." Bart said.

Hawk took one look at the portly black man who managed the tent shack. He took another look at his companion, then at Gruff. Gruff Garrett stared right at Hawk and did not waver. He didn't say anything, but he didn't need to. His quiet, steel gaze only reinforced what he had said earlier. Gruff wasn't out here looking for trouble, but he was more than capable of handling himself, if it came up. That was Hawk's last warning.

The old man took a moment to pause, and suddenly reason and sense came back to him. He blinked and shook his head. "Never mind." he said, simply as he slinked back to his long table.

Hawk seemed to mumble something as he went back to sit down, but Gruff couldn't make out what he said. He didn't care for whatever it was. He was just glad that the old man saw reason in the end. Gruff had already been in one skirmish earlier, and he was in no mood to be in another, so soon after.

Gruff was relieved that the tension was cut so easily and nothing came of it. If he still had his youth, Gruff might have relished the chance to get into a fight with Hawk, but he was not a young man anymore. He was really getting too old for sudden and pointless confrontations like that, and he would rather avoid a fight than get into one.

"Sorry about Hawk back there. Don't mind him. He just gets all nuts when he gets a little drunk. Which is quite often." Bart said.

"Forget it. A man like that is going to get into trouble on his own account. That's his business. I just don't want to be there when it happens. I just want to finish this final job of mine, and well, do whatever retired US Marshals do when they retire."

"Final job? You're going to pick up that prisoner of the mayor?"

Gruff nodded. "How did you know?"

Bart shrugged his shoulders. "Just a lucky guess. I

figured what else would an old marshal be doing in this little mining town?"

"You're a perceptive one, yeah."

"In a small town like this? You gotta be perceptive and then some. You can sleep in the third cot, in the next tent. It's pretty comfortable if I do say so myself. Just hand my boy fifty cents."

Gruff nodded and got up from the table. He walked out of the tent and towards the other tent that Bart had mentioned. There was a young black boy standing in front, just as he said.

"Fifty cents for a cot, Sir." he said.

Gruff handed the coins to the young boy without saying a word and entered the tent.

Gruff entered the tent and saw some men sleeping on some of the cots. Just as Bart had said, the third cot in the tent was empty. Gruff moved towards the cot and lay down to get some sleep.

It only took Gruff a few moments to lie on the cot before sleep came to him. A younger Gruff Garrett would have actually had a more difficult time to get sleep. In his younger days, Gruff was one to sleep with one eye open, and one hand on his revolver. Gruff was always one to have shallow sleep, and to be ready and alert for any kind of trouble that might pop up. That was a time when he was much younger, and his body was much stronger. Gruff didn't tire as easily, and he didn't need to rest so deeply. Now, he was an older man, and his older body craved desperately for rest when it could get it.

He fell into a deep slumber and the first thing he saw was Katie. She was looking down at him and smiling. He saw her young and pretty face again, and the old lawdog's old ticker was filled with joy. Katie seemed to be glowing with a warm glow that radiated absolute peace and happiness.

"Katie. Katie, it's really you! You're here!" he said.

Katie smiled and nodded. "Of course I'm here, Gruff. I'm always watching you. I couldn't just leave an old galoot like yourself like that."

Somehow at the back of Gruff's sleeping mind, he knew that this was all a dream. Somehow, he knew that this was all not real, but he welcomed it anyway. He was more than happy to stay in this fantasy that his mind had concocted while he was sleeping. It was definitely more desirable than his real life now.

"You… you didn't leave me? Then that means, that means you're all right? You're good, ain't you? You're fine. That's all I ever really wanted for you. That you be fine." Gruff said.

Katie was about to say something to Gruff. Perhaps she was going to reassure him, that she was fine. Perhaps she was going to give him some kind of nugget of wisdom, some tantalizing proof that she was still very well, despite having passed on. Whatever it was, she wouldn't get the chance. Gruff watched in horror as a man snuck up behind Katie and pointed a gun behind her head.

"Katie! No, not again! No!" /Gruff was filled with panic and desperation. It was happening again. Katie was going to get shot and there was nothing he could do about it.

Gruff opened his eyes and looked up from the cot he

lay on. Katie was gone now. The dream had faded away and he was back in reality. However, he saw that he was staring down the barrel of the gun. The man was who was pointing a gun down at him was the same man who was pointing his gun at Katie in his dream. Somehow, the dream had bled into reality.

Gruff's eyes were wide with terror as he called out for Katie. "Katie, no!"

The man with the gun looked down at Gruff with a look of confusion. He was staring down at Gruff as if he were a man who was not all there. In a sense, perhaps he was right.

"Whoa. I thought you were someone else. Sorry partner. Wouldn't want to shoot a man who had nothing to do with my troubles." the man said.

He pulled back his gun and Gruff slowly settled down to waking up. Gruff wasn't sure how long he had been asleep. He hoped that he had slept well and long enough, and that the morning was close. He didn't like the feeling of being mistaken for someone else, and having a gun pointed at him, but Gruff tried not to think about it too much. After all, this was a mining town, and mining towns were always rough and rowdy. This one was probably no different from just about any other mining town out there. It was probably just even more reinforcement of what Gruff already knew in his heart. He was getting too old for this kind of job.

"I can't wait to get out of here and finish this job." he said to himself.

Chapter Six: Chewing on the Bone

Gruff didn't bother to try and get some sleep again. He looked out and checked and saw that it was early enough. Bart was already up, and Gruff had him prepare a full breakfast of coffee, flapjacks, and ham. He ate well and hardy. Gruff knew that he would probably need all the energy he could get.

After paying Bart for everything, he proceeded to the livery stable where he fetched Dynamite. This was as good a time as any to get going.

Gruff swung by the mayor's office and saw that Mathers was awake. "Good morning. As promised, I'll be taking the prisoner and paying you, your reward." Gruff said.

Mathers nodded. "Thank goodness. I was getting tired of his jabbering all this time. Good to see you also took care of those mountain men. I had the undertaker sweep the bodies off of the jailhouse too."

Gruff nodded and they proceeded to the old, makeshift jailhouse. Paolo Dixon was there wide awake. A wide grin was plastered on his face. His smiling countenance only seemed to annoy Mathers even more.

"Well, slap these on him, so I can get him out of your hair." Gruff said.

He handed Mathers a tight pair of handcuffs. Mathers took them, and unlocked the cell door. Even before he opened the door, Gruff already had his gun pulled out, and pointed at Dixon. He made sure there would be no more unwanted surprises, and said as much.

"Put 'em on, Dixon. Don't try nothing stupid and let's get this over with." Gruff said.

Dixon kept his smile and stretched out both his wrists. "My word. You hurt my feelings, Gruff. I had nothing to do with those mountain men attacking yesterday and you should know me well enough by now. I'm not going to try anything stupid, man. I ain't like that. But like I said yesterday. This be your last jogo, both of you's! My gang, the Poison club is coming for me, an' you'll both be dancing the dance of death!"

"Shut yer trap with the dancing and the voodoo horse manure already!" Mathers said.

"Ain't no confirmation that his gang really is coming

after him, Mayor?" Gruff asked.

Mathers shook his head. "Don't be spooked by Dixon's antics. You've already gotten this far to fetch him. I shouldn't even be tellin' you that. A grizzled, old lawdog like yourself should know when someone is just talking and all bluster."

Gruff felt a little ashamed at what Mathers pointed out. There was no reason to put any credence to Dixon's words. The light of the dawn would come soon, and it was just time for them to go. The mountains and a long trek were beckoning.

Mathers slapped the handcuffs on Dixon with no incident.

"All right. Get moving." Gruff said.

He poked Dixon with the barrel of his gun, and they walked him to his horse that had already been hitched nearby. Dixon's horse looked even hardier and healthier than Gruff's steed. These animals would serve them both well for the long trip ahead. Before he got on the horse, Gruff promptly paid Mathers. The sight of all the greenbacks made the old bounty hunter, mayor and dentist all rolled into one smile.

"Finally. Now it was all worth it."

"You ain't going to be smiling like that when my gang comes a' ridin' here!"

"Shut up and get on your horse already. Get ready for a long ride back." Gruff said.

Dixon got up and Gruff got on Dynamite, as well. The trail loomed ahead of them. They both felt the cold air of the morning on them, and the trail seemed quite enough. The mountains were right in front of them, a large path of green as far as the eye could see. It was time to ride out.

They had been riding for three hours without saying a word to each other. The horses were moving at a casual, but deliberate trot. Gruff didn't want to ride them too hard. There was still a long way to go, and there would be no point in pushing the animals too early. Gruff had his eyes and ears peeled through the whole trip. He was quiet, but his entire body was ready to spur into action, if he needed to. Gruff still had not completely dismissed what Dixon had been yapping about all this time. There was still the disturbing possibility that his gang was coming after him, and he had to be ready for that.

It was Gruff who broke the silence and asked a question. "How many desperadoes are in your gang?"

Dixon looked a little surprised by his question. He thought about the answer before speaking. "Well, there's Nic Matias, Dave Krebeck, Lannie Bolton, and Ken Thorn to name a few. There were some other stragglers there too. Mostly friends of those four I mentioned."

"How many "friends of those four" did you manage to recruit? How many were you in all?"

"I'd say around twenty-two, more or less."

From the names that Dixon had rattled off, Matias and Krebeck were the worrisome ones. Gruff had heard of the two outlaws and they were known to be pretty ornery. If Dixon did have them in the gang, that would definitely be trouble. And dealing with more than twenty men would not be something Gruff was looking forward to.

"I think we're being followed." Gruff said, plainly.

"You think so? What makes you say that?" Dixon asked.

He sounded a little more surprised than he should have been. "I don't know. Just my instincts. Could be, or maybe not. Either way, I've learned to trust my instincts. They're the ones that have kept me alive all these years, anyway."

"I ain't arguin' with that."

"Tell you what. We've been riding for three hours straight. Despite a good and hearty breakfast, I'm starting to get a little hungry. Must be my age, or the tension, or both. Let's set up camp and rest a bit. We should recharge just a mite, but I'll be listening and watching for anything." Gruff said.

"All right. If that's what you want. I could sure use some refreshment myself."

"You'll get some nourishment, but not much. Just enough for you to last for the whole ride."

"Why thank you, Gruff! I didn't know you cared for me, that much."

Gruff ignored Dixon's sarcasm and pulled on Dynamite's reins. The horse stopped as well as Dixon's. Gruff got down first, then pulled out a pair of leg irons from his saddlebags. The leg irons looked pretty heavy and cumbersome.

"Put 'em on." Gruff said.

"I really won't be needing to wear those. I mean, where would I go now and..."

"I said, put 'em on." Garrett's tone was firm. He wasn't going to repeat himself. Dixon wasn't going to have a choice in the matter. He took the leg irons and snapped them on his ankles. He immediately felt their cumbersome weight on him. Walking would be a chore with these on, and running away was simply out of the question.

The two men settled down, and Gruff brewed two cups of coffee for them. He handed Dixon his cup along with some biscuits to go with it. Dixon was pleased with the small snack.

"That's the best coffee I've tasted in a long while! I gotta say, Mathers never could brew a good cup, but I never knew you could! You shoulda' taken another job brewin' coffee!"

"Glad you like it. We're both going to need the energy."

"You know, seeing as you brewed me a great cup of coffee for the morning, and how we're riding together, I might as well come clean with you. There really isn't anything more I can do, considering just how bull-headed you are. Ain't no way you're letting me out of your sight. And the way you manhandled those mountain men, yesterday? I can see that you're really serious about seeing this whole thing through, no matter what. For whatever reason."

"Of course I am. Now what is this all about? What do you have to tell me?"

"It's about my gang. They're not really coming to rescue me. They're coming after me. They want to kill me."

"They're coming after you, eh? So you double-crossed them?"

"Well, yeah. It's kinda what I do, man."

"Well, ain't that a surprise."

Garrett wasn't really surprised at this new revelation. He knew Dixon well enough by now, to know that he was naturally a double-crossing snake. It wasn't surprising that he had made a lot of enemies, including his own gang. That was just Paolo Dixon for you. You just couldn't trust him, and he wasn't one to make any lasting friendships or allies.

"I just wanted to tell you up front, man. These boys o' mine, they be merciless. They will not hesitate to kill you to get to me. I'm telling you now, it would be best if you just let me go an' I can take my chances with 'em."

Gruff snickered. "Nice try, Dixon. Why would I let you go? I came here to finish my job, an' that's exactly what I'm going to do."

"Why would you let me go? Well for starters, they ain't got no beef with you, man. They got beef with me. You let me go, there ain't no reason for them to kill you. If they stumble onto me, you can just go on back home, with no more issue, no more problems. There would be no reason for them to kill you. But if you stick with me well, you know."

"They hate you that much so they would kill anyone who would come between them an' you. I kinda understand the feeling."

Dixon sneered. "Ohhh, that's cold man. Real cold."

Gruff shook his head and took another sip of his coffee. "That ain't cold. That's just the truth. An' the truth is also what I've been saying since I got here. I got a job to do. And my job is to get you back to the fort where you can face a proper trial for all the stuff you done. I aim to finish the job, no matter what."

Dixon shook his head. "I can't say that I'm not surprised. I've known you long enough to know that you're a stubborn old man. When you set your mind to something, you want to see it through, to the end. Like a dog chewing on a bone an' not letting go."

"I have been known to be pretty hard-headed. But that's just who I am, Dixon."

Dixon shook his head and whistled. A look of disappointment came over him. "Well, you can't say I didn't warn you, Gruff. When they come find us, and mind you they will. When they find us, you're a dead man."

Gruff smiled. "I'm pretty ancient. I've lived a lot longer than I should have. If I die doing my job well, so be it. I've lived and done enough. Maybe that would just be the best way to go. Maybe that's just the way it has to be."